This book belongs to

W9-AUO-290

Esther Shriner

Budding Ballerina!
2019

To Sonali
—GM

For Liliane, Sandra,
and Tomo T. Bergère
—CC

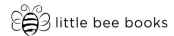 little bee books

A division of Bonnier Publishing
853 Broadway, New York, New York 10003
Text copyright © 2016 by Bonnier Publishing
Illustrations copyright © 2016 by Célia Chauffrey
All rights reserved, including the right of reproduction in whole
or in part in any form. LITTLE BEE BOOKS is a trademark
of Bonnier Publishing Group, and associated colophon is a
trademark of Bonnier Publishing Group.
Manufactured in China   LEO 0716
First Edition   10 9 8 7 6 5 4 3 2 1
ISBN 978-1-4998-0281-8

littlebeebooks.com
bonnierpublishing.com

Library of Congress Cataloging-in-Publication Data:
Names: Maccarone, Grace, adaptor. | Chauffrey, Célia, illustrator. |
Hoffmann, E. T. A. (Ernst Theodor Amadeus), 1776-1822. Nussknacker und Mausekönig.
Title: The Nutcracker / adapted by Grace Maccarone ; illustrated by Célia Chauffrey.
Description: New York : Little Bee Books, [2016] | Summary: Relates the story of the popular ballet
in which a little girl's love for the Nutcracker brings him to life.
Identifiers: LCCN 2015049670 | ISBN 9781499802818 (hardback)
Subjects: | CYAC: Fairy tales. | Christmas—Fiction. | BISAC: JUVENILE FICTION / Fairy Tales & Folklore / Adaptations. |
JUVENILE FICTION / Holidays & Celebrations / Christmas & Advent. | JUVENILE FICTION / Toys, Dolls, Puppets.
Classification: LCC PZ8.M1708 Nut 2016 | DDC [E]—dc23
LC record available at https://lccn.loc.gov/2015049670

# The Nutcracker

adapted by
Grace Maccarone

illustrated by
Célia Chauffrey

little bee books

Waiting behind closed doors was difficult for Clara and Fritz. But it was especially difficult on Christmas Eve!

The children struggled to avoid wrinkling and spotting their new clothes. Clara was able to meet the challenge, but Fritz found it unbearable.

Clara and her brother tried to busy themselves with their favorite books, but the activity behind the doors drew all their attention. Neither Robin Hood's nor Alice's adventures could pull them away.

Only the loudest sounds came through the solidly built walls and door. "I bet that's one of your presents," said the mischief-making Fritz at the sound of a sudden crash. "It's probably broken."

Seven-year-old Clara, though, was used to her brother's taunts and was not concerned. Especially since she was absorbed by imaginings of her own. Behind the doors, she envisioned a tree with toys and edible treats, and beneath the tree, a large box containing a new doll, curly-haired, in a dress with a big sash and pantaloons with many layers. Oh, how lovely she would be! They'd go on excursions and be constant companions—the very best of friends.

Meanwhile, Fritz hoped for more soldiers to strengthen his army for imaginary battles to come.

The doors opened to the biggest tree the family ever had. Apples, nuts, and candles dressed its branches, and below were boxes, beautifully wrapped and ribboned.

The door chimes announced aunts, uncles, cousins, and friends. They wore satin, silk, taffeta, and velvet in hues of emerald green, sapphire blue, ruby red, silver, and gold.

The dancing began—waltz, polka, mazurka, and polonaise. The angel on top of the tree, had she been real, would have seen the dancers arrange and rearrange themselves like colorful glass pieces in a kaleidoscope.

But amidst all this excitement, Clara nearly failed to notice that someone important was missing—Godfather Drosselmeyer.

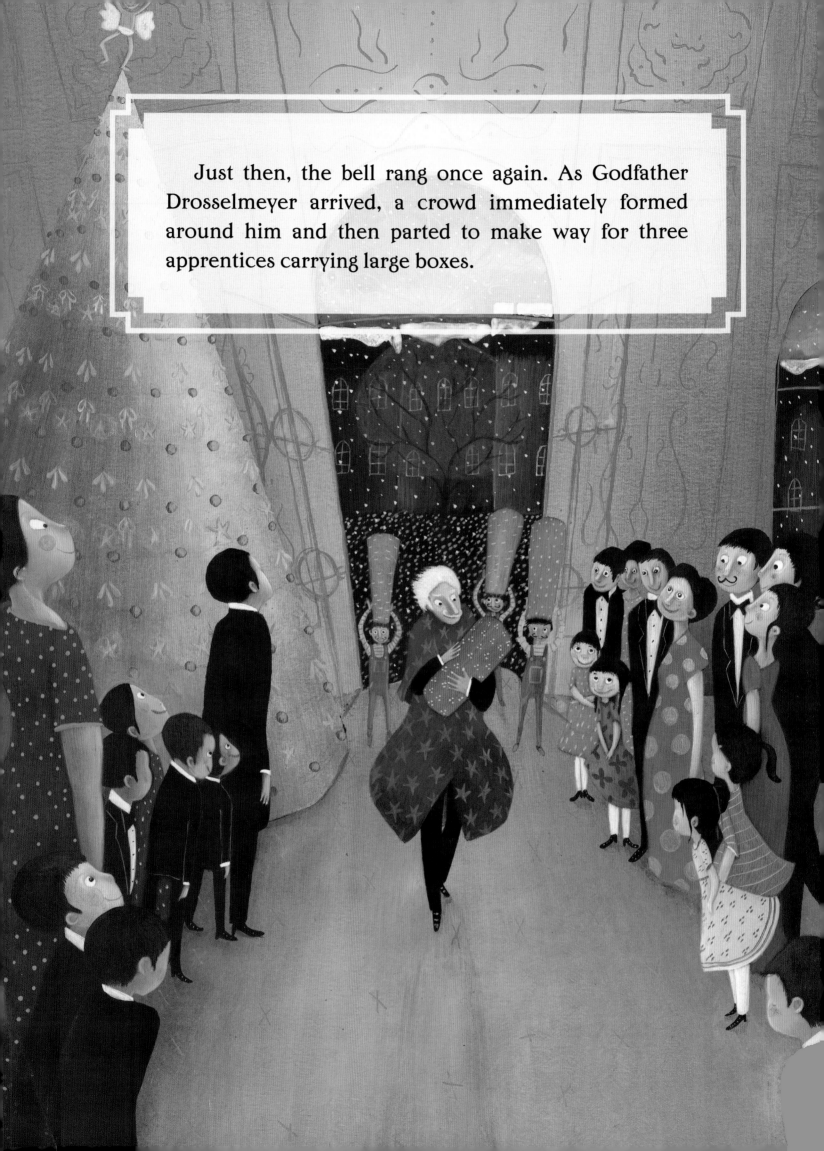

Just then, the bell rang once again. As Godfather Drosselmeyer arrived, a crowd immediately formed around him and then parted to make way for three apprentices carrying large boxes.

All conversation stopped as the apprentices set down the boxes and Drosselmeyer opened them one-by-one to reveal life-size mechanical dolls—a soldier, a ballerina, and a clown. Drosselmeyer wound them up, and they seemed to come to life.

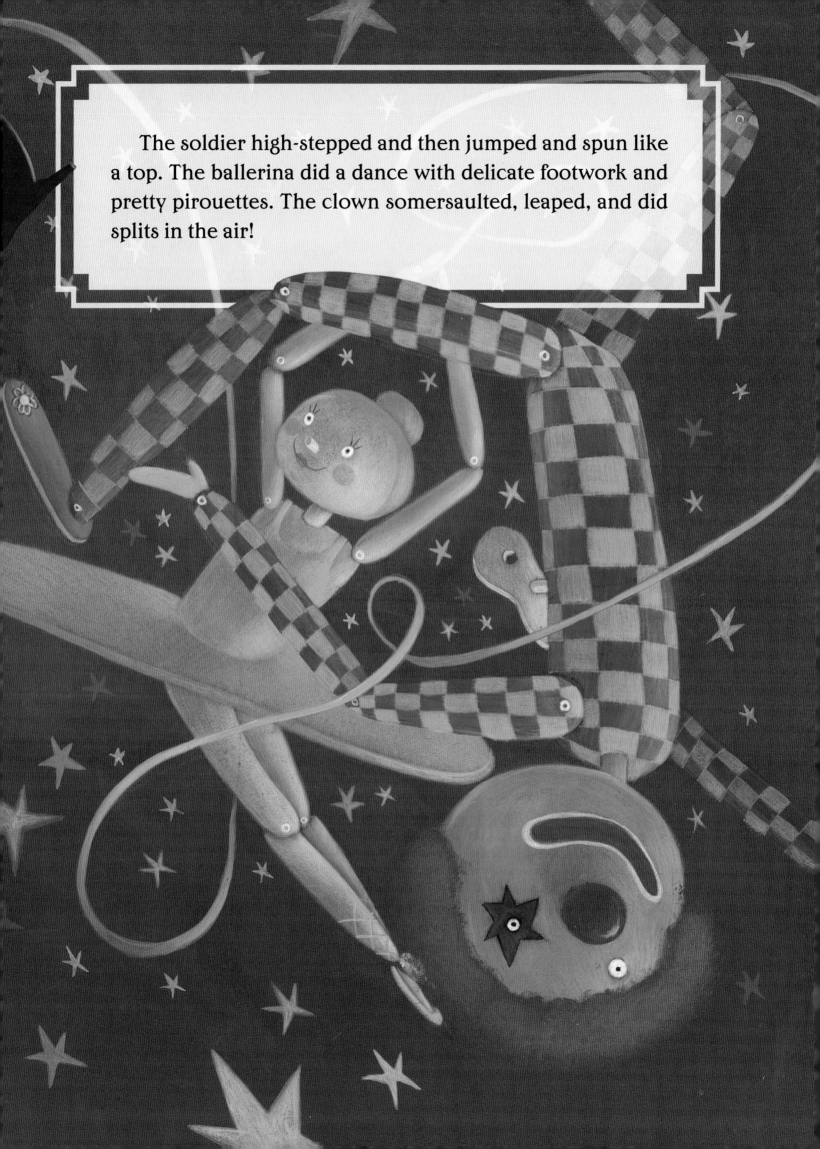

The soldier high-stepped and then jumped and spun like a top. The ballerina did a dance with delicate footwork and pretty pirouettes. The clown somersaulted, leaped, and did splits in the air!

When the show was over, Drosselmeyer had one more toy to share. It was made of wood and dressed like a soldier. But its head was overly large, and the wooden soldier exposed its teeth like a smiling chimp.

Godfather Drosselmeyer put a nut between those teeth and pressed a lever behind the soldier's neck. The nut, now free of its shell, went directly into Drosselmeyer's mouth.

Every child in the room had a chance to try this unusual toy and to eat a nut too.

After the children had their fill of nuts, they drifted off to explore other toys and games.

Only Clara could see beyond the useful function and homely face to a soul that was good and kind. Taking possession of the Nutcracker, Clara cradled it in her arms as if it were a baby doll.

But Fritz, always ready to stir up excitement, had been watching. He grabbed the Nutcracker from his sister and ran.

Blocked by Fritz's army of bugle-blowing cousins, Clara wasn't able to free her Nutcracker from Fritz's clumsy grasp.

Fritz dropped the Nutcracker, and it broke. Clara fell to her knees and wept.

But Godfather Drosselmeyer, who had witnessed the scene, came to the rescue. He replaced the Nutcracker's dislocated jaw and secured it with a handkerchief.

After dinner was eaten and packages were unwrapped, the guests resumed dancing until their legs wobbled. Then the clock struck twelve—Christmas Eve had passed and Christmas Day had begun.

The guests departed, tired but happy.

Dressed for bed, Clara had returned to the drawing room to take one more look at the tree and to say goodnight to the Nutcracker, when something surprising happened.

The tree—along with everything else in the room—grew before her very eyes. Then . . .

Fritz's toy soldiers snapped into action and defended their territory. Joining them, the Nutcracker fought the biggest mouse of all: the one with the golden crown.

Though strong and brave, the Nutcracker was overwhelmed. So without any regard for her own safety, Clara threw herself at the Mouse King, who flicked her away like a tiny fly.

Clara removed her shoe and threw it with all her might.
She hit the Mouse King on the head, and he fell at once.
The mice, taking their leader's stiff body with them, retreated.

But it was too late. The Nutcracker lay motionless on the ground. Clara placed her head on his wooden chest and sobbed.

Beneath her head, Clara felt a sudden softness and warmth. She looked at the Nutcracker's face and saw that it had been transformed—the wood was now flesh; the painted features were now dimensional eyes, nose, lips, and teeth. And they were much prettier.

Just then, Godfather Drosselmeyer stood before her. Had he been present all along? Drosselmeyer introduced the boy as his nephew, Hans-Peter, who had been under the wicked spell of Queen Mouseling, mother of the Mouse King.

With love and courage, Clara had broken the spell.

Drosselmeyer led Clara and Hans-Peter to a magical sleigh that transported the threesome through the sky. They passed over an enchanted forest where snowflakes danced.

The sleigh arrived in the Land of Sweets, where Godfather Drosselmeyer introduced the children to the Sugarplum Fairy.

Dancers from faraway lands entertained Clara and Hans-Peter and gave them tasty treats. Spanish dancers gave the children marzipan stars and performed an energetic flamenco. Dancers from Sri Lanka gave the children tea and then did a peacock dance.

African dancers, with gifts of chocolate, performed a dance of celebration and joy. They were followed by Brazilian dancers who came with coffee and did a rhythmical samba. Japanese kabuki dancers gave the children sweet mochi, and Russian tropak dancers gave them halvah.

When the dancing was over, the Sugarplum Fairy crowned Clara and Hans-Peter queen and king of the Land of Sweets.

Godfather Drosselmeyer reappeared and took the children on a sleepy voyage home.

Clara awoke to the sound of door chimes. She was in the drawing room with everything back to normal size. The only difference was that her beloved Nutcracker was nowhere to be seen. Clara started to cry.

Then she peeked behind the door.

# Selected Bibliography

*Books*

Balanchine, George, and Francis Mason. *101 Stories of the Great Ballets*. Garden City: Doubleday & Company, Inc., 1954, 1968, 1975.

Hoffmann, E.T.A. *Nutcracker*. Illustrated by Maurice Sendak. Trans. Ralph Manheim. New York: Crown Publishers, Inc., 1984.

Verdy, Violette. Illustrated by Marcia Brown. *Of Swans, Sugarplums and Satin Slippers: Ballet Stories for Children*. New York: Scholastic, 1991.

*Electronic Sources*

Dumas père, Alexandre. *Histoire d'un casse-noisette*. Paris: J. Hetzel, 1845. Gallica Bibliothèque Numérique. June 28, 2010. July 5, 2015. http://gallica.bnf.fr/ark:/12148/btv1b86002949/f5.image.r=Histoire%20d%27un%20casse-noisette,%20par%20Alexandre.langEN

Hoffmann, E.T.A. *Nussknacker und Mausekönig*. 1816. Berlin. Spiegel Online Kultur. Projekt Gutenberg-DE. http://gutenberg.spiegel.de/buch/-3083/1

Hoffmann, E.T.A. *Nutcracker and Mouse-king*. Trans. Mrs. St Simon. New York: D. Appleton & Company, 1852. Internet Archive. University of North Carolina at Chapel Hill. March 2, 2012. July 5, 2015. https://archive.org/details/nutcrackermousek00hoff

*Video Recordings*

*George Balanchine's The Nutcracker*. Dir. Emile Ardolino. Perf. New York City Ballet, Macaulay Culkin. DVD. Warner Home Video, 1993.

*The Nutcracker*. Dir. Andreas Morrell. Perf. The Mariinsky Ballet and Orchestra. DVD. Warner Classics, 2012.

*The Nutcracker*. Dir. Roger M. Sherman, Ross MacGibbon. Perf. Anthony Dowell, Alina Cojocaru, The Royal Ballet. DVD. Opus Arte, 2001.

*The Nutcracker*. Dir. Tony Charmoli. Perf. The American Ballet Theatre, Mikhail Baryshnikov. VHS. MGM/UA Home Video, 1977.

*Music Recordings*

Ellington, Duke. "Tchaikovsky: The Nutcracker." *Three Suites*. Columbia Jazz Masterpieces, 1990. (A jazz interpretation.)

Tchaikovsky, Pyotr Ilych (Composer). *The Nutcracker*. Perf. Valery Gergiev and the Kirov Orchestra and Choir. CD. Decca, 1998.